# Five reasons why we think you'll love this book!

## Winnie AND Wilbur
## THE AMAZING PUMPKIN

This book will make you love your veggies!

You can take the Winnie and Wilbur challenge: can you find a duck?

There is so much to spot in every picture.

Winnie talks about a friend of hers who you might know, too!

You can join in when Winnie shouts 'Abracadabra!'

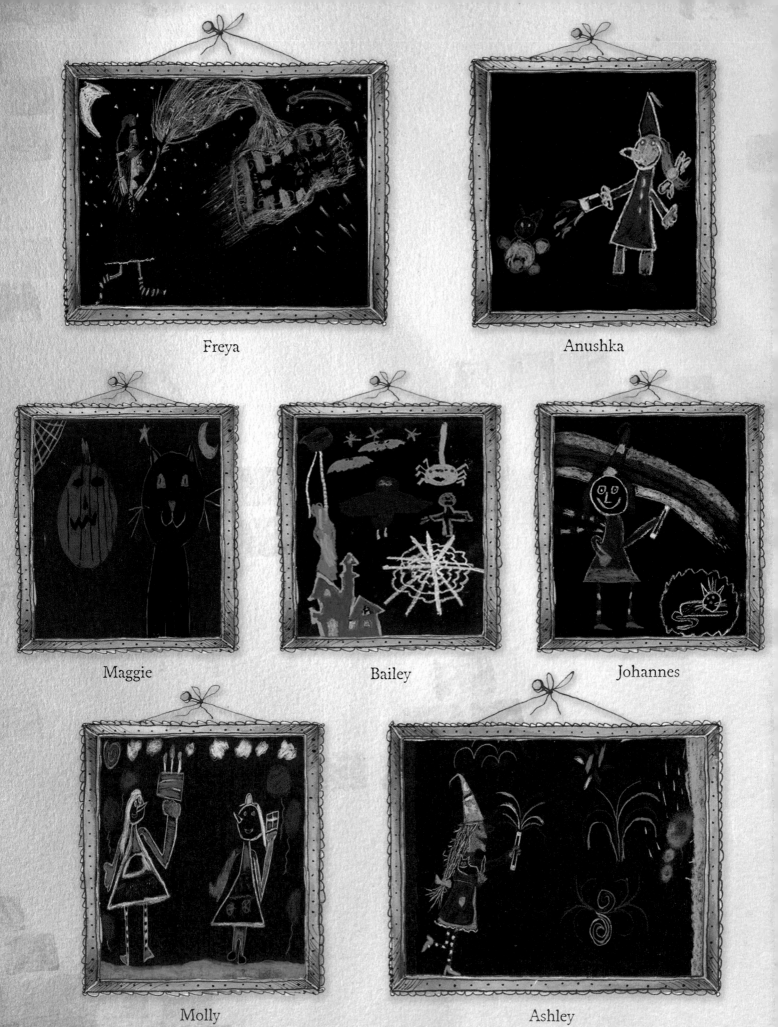

Freya

Anushka

Maggie

Bailey

Johannes

Molly

Ashley

Amber

Jun-Yeong

Pablo

Matilda

Marwin

Hasan

Rebecca

Thank you to all these schools for helping
with the endpapers:

St Barnabas Primary School, Oxford; St Ebbe's Primary
School, Oxford; Marcham Primary School, Abingdon; St
Michael's C.E. Aided Primary School, Oxford; St Bede's
RC Primary School, Jarrow; The Western Academy,
Beijing, China; John King School, Pinxton; Neston
Primary School, Neston; Star of the Sea RC Primary
School, Whitley Bay; José Jorge Letria Primary School,
Cascais, Portugal; Dunmore Primary School, Abingdon;
Özel Bahçeşehir İlköğretim Okulu, Istanbul, Turkey; the
International School of Amsterdam, the Netherlands;
Princethorpe Infant School, Birmingham.

For Margaret Shewan, to celebrate
her 70th birthday—V.T.

For Helen Mortimer—K.P.

## OXFORD
### UNIVERSITY PRESS

Great Clarendon Street, Oxford OX2 6DP

Oxford University Press is a department of the University of Oxford.
It furthers the University's objective of excellence in research, scholarship,
and education by publishing worldwide. Oxford is a registered trade mark of
Oxford University Press in the UK and in certain other countries

Text copyright © Valerie Thomas 2009
Illustrations copyright © Korky Paul 2009, 2016
The moral rights of the author and artist
have been asserted

Database right Oxford University Press (maker)

First published as *Winnie's Amazing Pumpkin* in 2009
This edition first published in 2016

British Library Cataloguing in Publication Data available

ISBN: 978-0-19-274820-1 (paperback)
ISBN: 978-0-19-274907-9 (paperback and CD)

10 9 8 7 6 5 4 3 2 1

Printed in China

Paper used in the production of this book is a natural, recyclable product made
from wood grown in sustainable forests. The manufacturing process conforms
to the environmental regulations of the country of origin

### www.winnieandwilbur.com

VALERIE THOMAS AND KORKY PAUL

# Winnie AND Wilbur
# THE AMAZING PUMPKIN

OXFORD

UNIVERSITY PRESS

Winnie the Witch ate lots of vegetables.

She liked broccoli, cauliflower,
cabbage, and parsnips.
She really liked peas, carrots,
beans, potatoes, and spinach.

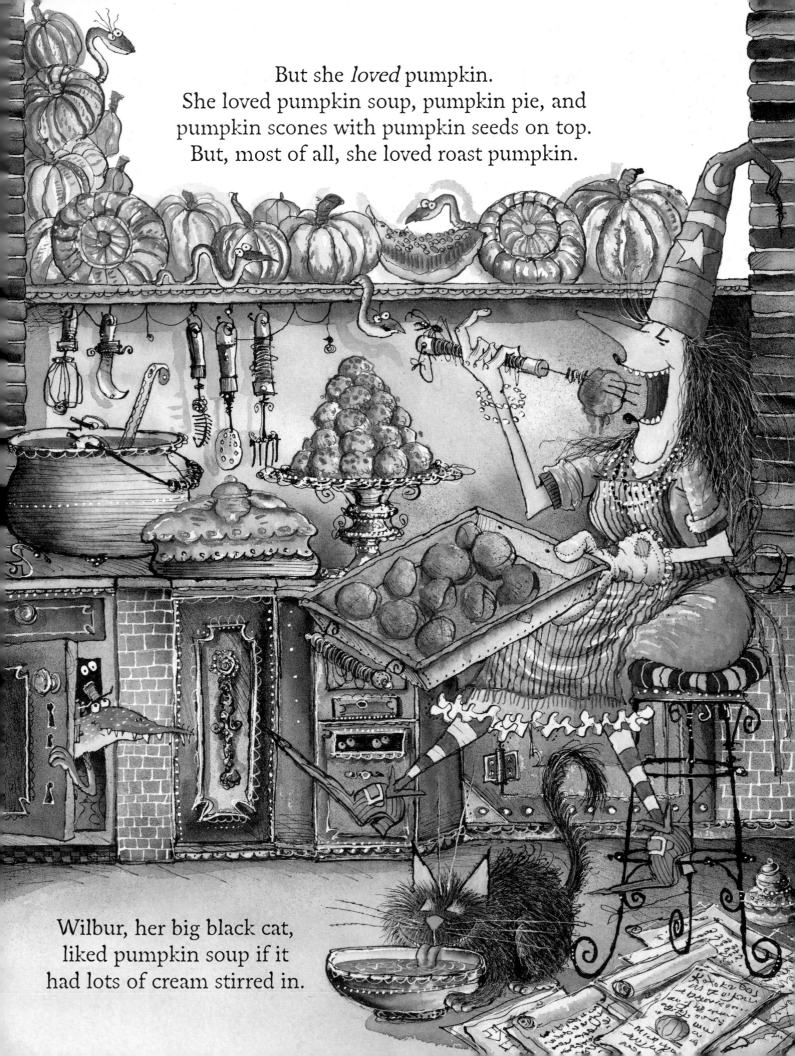

But she *loved* pumpkin.
She loved pumpkin soup, pumpkin pie, and
pumpkin scones with pumpkin seeds on top.
But, most of all, she loved roast pumpkin.

Wilbur, her big black cat,
liked pumpkin soup if it
had lots of cream stirred in.

Every Saturday morning Winnie
would jump onto her broomstick,
Wilbur would jump onto her
shoulder, and they would zoom
off to the farmers' market
to buy their vegetables.

That was easy.

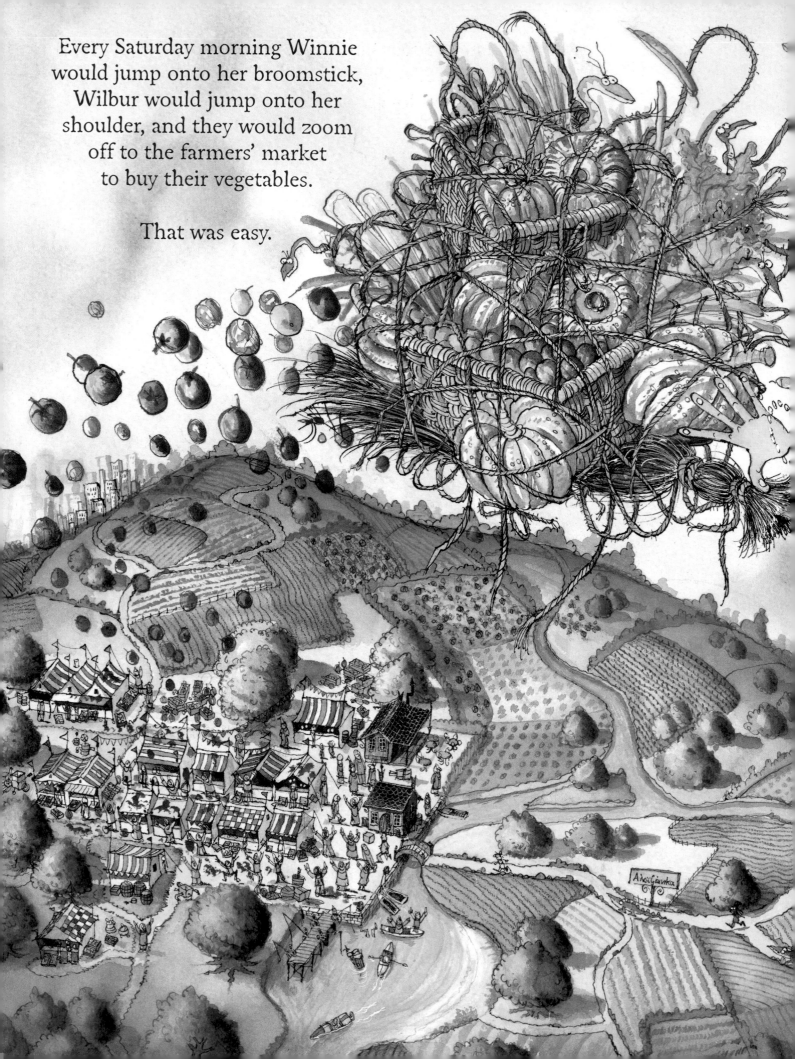

But it wasn't so easy coming home.
It is hard to balance on a broomstick with
a cat, pumpkins, and lots of other vegetables.

**Ooops!** Brussels sprouts and tomatoes
rained down on the market.

Splat! Squelch!

'Blithering broomsticks!' shouted Winnie.
And then she had a good idea.

'I'll grow my own vegetables,' she said.
So Winnie dug a big vegetable patch
in her garden.

Wilbur helped.

She planted lots and lots of vegetables.
She watered the plants and pulled up
the weeds.

Wilbur helped.

But the plants grew very slowly.

And, when they did grow, the caterpillars
and snails and rabbits ate them.

'Oh dear,' said Winnie. 'Gardening is hard work.
I'll try a spell to help my garden grow.'

She waved her magic wand, shouted,

'Abracadabra!'

and nothing happened.

'Bother!' said Winnie.
'That didn't work.
I'll go and look in my
Big Book of Spells.'

Winnie went inside
just a minute too soon.

Outside, the spell
began to work.

Inside, it was very dark.
Winnie tripped over Wilbur.
**'Meooowww!'**
'I'm sorry, Wilbur,' said Winnie,
'I didn't see you. It's so dark, there
must be a storm on the way.'

She looked out of the window.
It wasn't a storm.
It was Winnie's garden.
The vegetables were growing so fast
they covered all the windows.

'I'd better go out and stop
the spell,' Winnie said.

But the door wouldn't open.
An enormous cabbage was in the way.

Winnie rushed upstairs, climbed
out of the bathroom window,
and slid down a giant beanstalk.

Wilbur climbed down behind her.
This is fun! he thought,
until he met a giant caterpillar.
**'Yeeoow!'**

Everything in Winnie's garden was
enormous, gigantic, stupendous!

A beanstalk was growing up into the clouds.
The cabbages were as big as cows.
The rabbits were bigger than cows.
An immense pumpkin vine was curling
around Winnie's house.

And there, on the roof, was a **huge** pumpkin.
'Oh no!' shouted Winnie.
'The pumpkin will squash my house!'
She waved her magic wand,
but just as she shouted . . .

'Abra . . .

# CRASH!

## . . . cadabra!'

the gigantic pumpkin
crashed to the ground.

Winnie's enormous, stupendous garden
shrank back to the way it was before.

But the pumpkin that had broken
off the vine was still a massive,
monstrous, amazing pumpkin.

Winnie chopped a doorway into the pumpkin.

She made pumpkin pies, pumpkin scones,
pumpkin soup with cream for Wilbur, and
an enormous dish of roast pumpkin.

But there was still lots of pumpkin left.

So she put a notice on the gate:

*FREE*
PUMPKIN

Help yourself...

People came with their bowls and
baskets and even wheelbarrows.

And soon the pumpkin shell was empty.

'What shall I do with the pumpkin shell?' wondered Winnie.
'It would make a good house, but I already have a house.

One of my friends once changed a pumpkin into a coach.
But that was for a special occasion.
And the horses might be a problem.'

Then Winnie had a wonderful idea. 'Yes!' she said. 'That's exactly what it looks like,' she said. 'Of course!'

She waved her magic wand, stamped her foot, shouted,

'Abracadabra!'

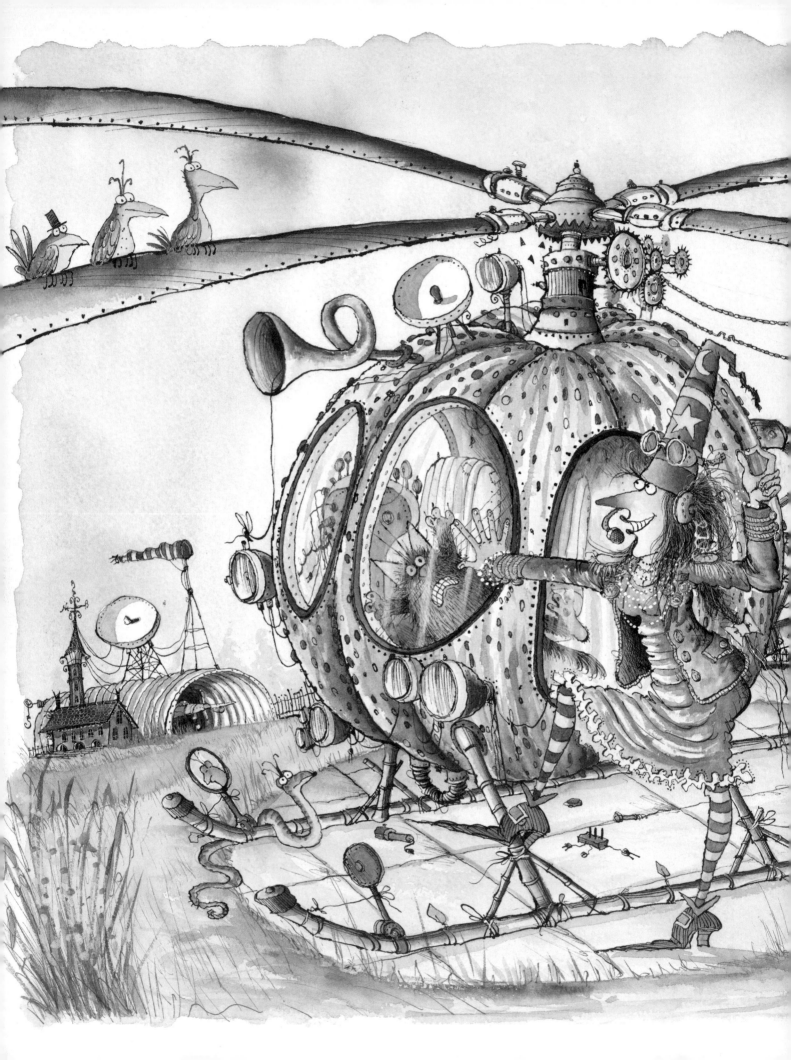

and there, in Winnie's garden,
was a bright orange helicopter.

So now, when Winnie and Wilbur go to the market,
Winnie can buy as many pumpkins as she likes.

And flying home in a helicopter is lots of fun!

Bethany

Katia

Eun-Jae

Kathleen

Ji-Eun

Jenny

Sara

Fraser

Ka Keung

Selin

Selin

Olivia

Siyabend

Kieran

# A note for grown-ups

Oxford Owl is a FREE and easy-to-use website packed with support and advice about everything to do with reading.

**Informative videos**

**Hints, tips and fun activities**

**Top tips from top writers for reading with your child**

**Help with choosing picture books**

For this expert advice and much, much more about how children learn to read and how to keep them reading ...

## LOOK
### for Oxford Owl
**www.oxfordowl.co.uk**